Library of Congress Cataloging-in-Publication Data

Clarke, Jane, 1954–
[Dance together dinosaurs]
Dancing with the Dinosaurs / written by Jane Clarke ; illustrated by Lee Wildish.
p. cm.
"An Imagine book."
Summary: From a tango by a T. Rex to a line dance with Danny Ig, dinosaurs demonstrate
their talents on Dancing with Dinosaurs, while the judges mysteriously disappear.
ISBN 978-1-936140-67-1 (hardcover)
[1. Stories in rhyme. 2. Dancing—Fiction. 3. Dinosaurs—Fiction.]
I. Wildish, Lee, ill. II. Title.
PZ8.3.C5484Dan 2012
[E]—dc23
2011024710

An Imagine Book
Published by Charlesbridge
85 Main Street
Watertown, MA 02472
(617) 926-0329
www.charlesbridge.com

First published in Great Britain in 2012 by Red Fox
An imprint of Random House Children's Books
A Random House Group Company

Printed in China

10 9 8 7 6 5 4 3 2 1

Printed and bound in October 2011 by Leo Paper Products in Heshan, China

For information about custom editions, special sales, premium and
corporate purchases, please contact Charlesbridge Publishing
at specialsales@charlesbridge.com

WRITTEN BY
Jane Clarke

ILLUSTRATED BY
Lee Wildish

imagine!
Publishing

Meet the contestants!

Our fang-tastic tyrannosaurus, T. Rex

Steggy Stegosaurus, our diamond-plated dancer

The Hadrosaur Duckbills are everything they're quacked-up to be

Be filled with rapture watching the raptors

Troodie is a truly talented troodon

Patty Apatosaurus is a whole heap of fun

Dancing comes tops with Tracey Triceratops

Kylie Ankylosaurus loves to dance when she's out clubbing

Barry Baryonyx is clawsome

Maia Maiasaurus is over the moon to be taking part

Donny Iguanodon gives dancing a thumbs-up

Spike Spinosaurus sticks out from the crowd

Lily Dilophosaurus is frilled to take part

Head bang with Pachycephalosaurus and the Bone-head Breakers

Dinosaurs, get ready!
Polish your fangs and claws,
   don't keep the judges waiting—
   come dancing with the 'saurs!

Tango with our
T. Rex,

do the **Steggy** twist and **shout!**

Disco with the Duckbills

and shake it all about.

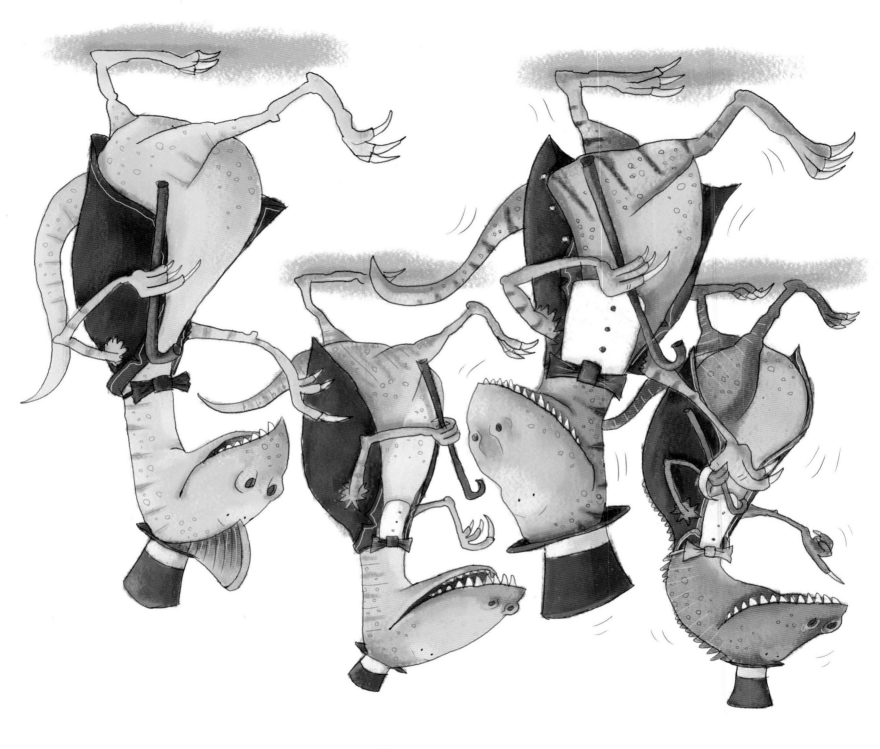

Tap along with raptors,

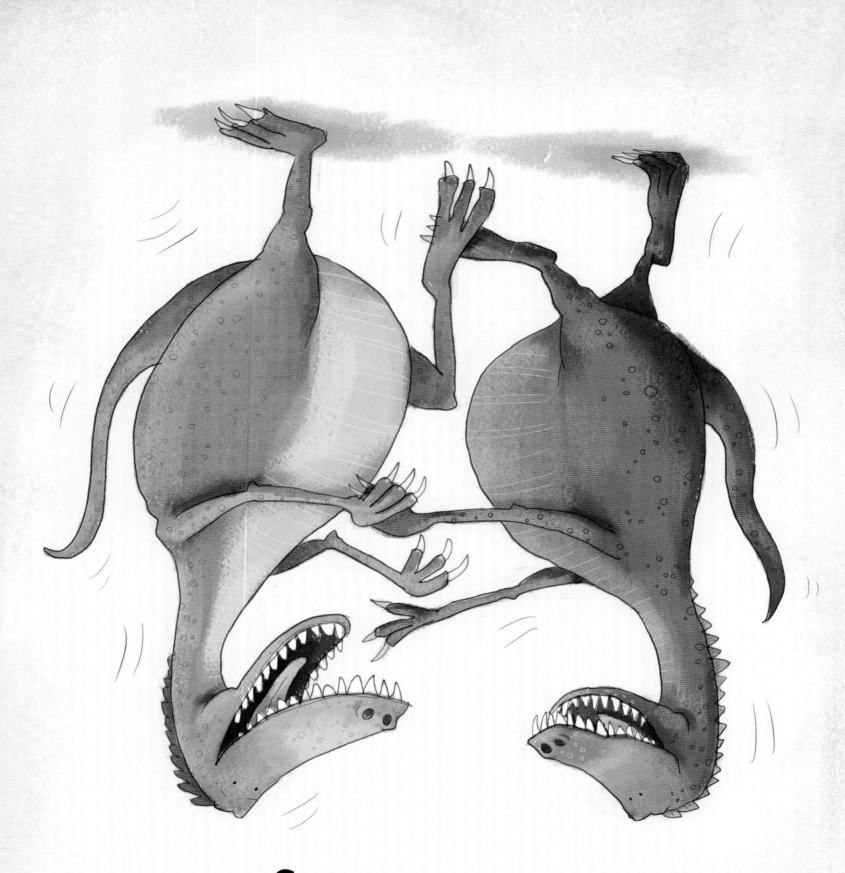

do the Troodie boogaloo,

stomp a 'saurus samba

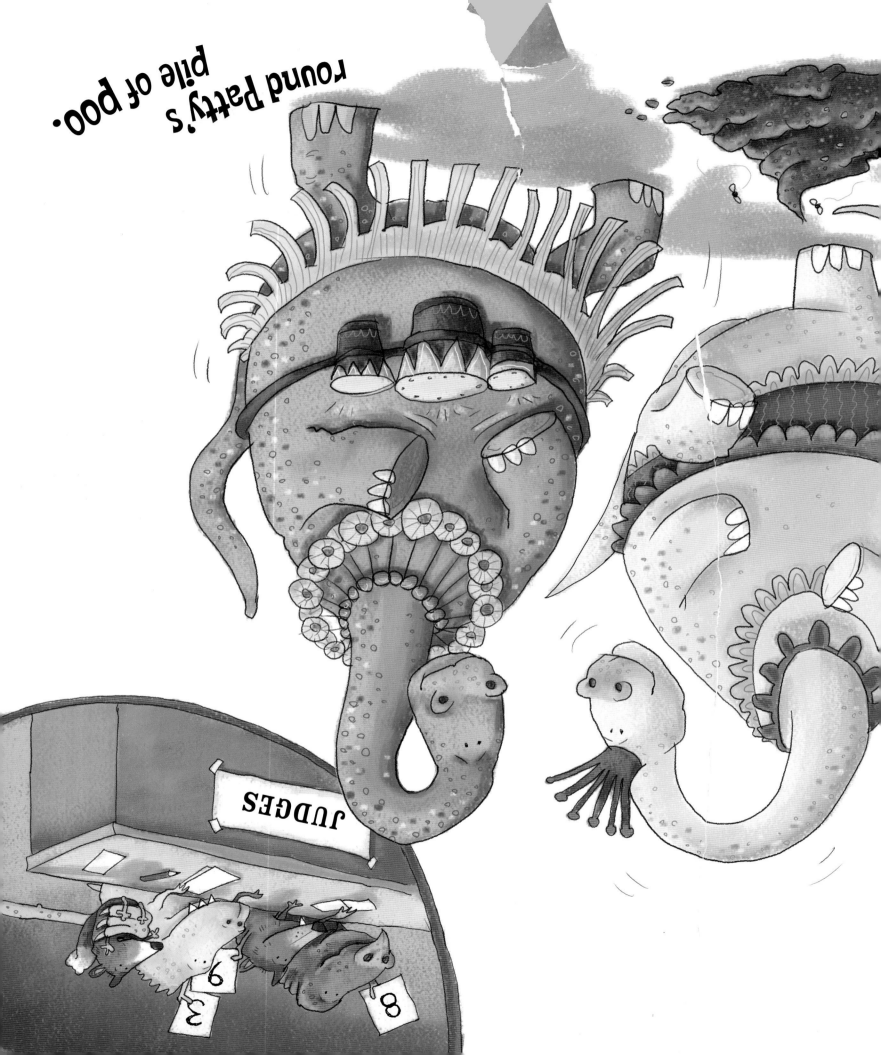

Body pop with Tracey Tops,

be swayed by **Barry's rumba,**

Cha-cha-cha with Kylie

in her great **big** sparkly number.

Moonwalk with **Miss Maia,**

step a Spike o'saurus jig,

put on your cowboy boots and hat,

waltz along with Lily,

join the All-saur All-stars ballet

wearing tights and something frilly.

Come on! Dance with dinosaurs!
You could be a winner!